I ♥
Selena Gomez

Harlee Harte

DOVE
B O O K S

I ♡
Selena Gomez

Copyright © 2009 Dove Books, Inc.

The opinions expressed in this book are those of the author of this book and do not necessarily reflect the views of the publisher or its affiliates.

ISBN-10: 1-59777-648-3
ISBN-13: 978-1-59777-648-6
Library of Congress Cataloging-In-Publication Data Available

Cover & Book Design by Sonia Fiore

Printed in the United States of America

Dove Books, Inc.
9465 Wilshire Boulevard, Suite 840
Beverly Hills, CA 90212

10 9 8 7 6 5 4 3 2 1

Collect all four
Harlee Harte books

I ♡ Taylor Swift

I ♡ The Jonas Brothers

I ♡ Selena Gomez

I ♡ Robert Pattinson

Hi!

I'm Harlee Harte.

I write the celebrity column, "HarteBeat," for the Hollywoodland High School newspaper. It's a blast! I get to meet and greet the hottest teen idols and hit the hip Tinseltown places to hang out and shop while I'm on the hunt. Being a columnist is hard work, but I just love the glamour and excitement! I'm always looking for the latest news about our favorite stars, so visit my Facebook page and see what I have going on or just say hello. My friends Kiki, Marcy, and Luzie pop in every now and then, too, and love to chime in on the latest fashions, cool beauty tips, music, celeb sightings, and advice on how to deal with parents, school, crushes, and friends.

I'd love to hear from you!

Harlee Harte

TABLE OF CONTENTS

PART ONE
The Assignment

"It was so fun at the beach, Harlee," whispered Kiki. "You should have been there." She slid over in her seat to let Marcy and Luzie squeeze in next to us.

"Are you trying to make me feel bad?" I said. "You know I couldn't go. Was he there?"

She nodded. "He" was the awesome Jack Kelly, my complete crush. "And Toby was there, and Joey, and Luzie, and…"

"Good morning, students!" Mrs. Marshall's overly cheery Monday morning voice cut through the excited weekend gossip, but didn't stop it. She cleared her throat. No effect. Finally she let loose with the microphone squeal that always brought an outraged silence to the auditorium, and all eyes turned towards her. She beamed from over the top of a ruffled pink shirt.

"I hope you are all ready for Give Back and Feel Good Week." She stood for a moment as if expecting a great burst of applause, or a drum roll, but was met instead by silence. She continued. "During this week of community service we will all think about how privileged we are at Hollywoodland High with our fine education and fancy clothes, and cell phones, and iPods." As if on cue, my cell phone started vibrating and ringing inside my Steve Madden bag. All I needed was for my iPod to blast out a tune, and we'd really get the picture. A wave of laughter started up from the rows around me, while all I could do was fumble to turn my phone to silent. I hoped that Mrs. Marshall wasn't able to figure out the guilty party.

No such luck. "You'll give that to me after assembly, Harlee. Even celebrity reporters should know to turn their phones off on arrival at school." She fixed me with a frown. "Last week you all came up with fund-raising ideas and thought about different charities, and this week you will decide on an appropriate charity to receive all the money you raise. Good luck to you all." She smiled at the whole school, then peered over the top of her glasses at me. "Oh, and Harlee, I'd like you to link this week's column for *The Hollywoodland Star* to this great event. To giving back. And feeling good. Now over to our special guest, Mr. Angus McTavish and his Scottish Bagpiping Troupe."

Great. No way I could write my column without my trusty cell phone. *How was I supposed to get the latest scoops texted right to me if my cell phone was sitting in the school principal's office?* That was embarrassing. And wrong. Just then my line of thought was drowned out by the tortured squeal of a dozen bagpipes. It would have to wait for later.

Lunch…

I was the first one at our table, so I sat and watched the lunchroom fill up, pretending I was people-watching at a Parisian café. Except it wasn't that glamorous as kids trailed in, grabbed their food, and sat down. Then my heart lurched and butterflies started turning somersaults in my stomach. Jack floated into view. I swear he had grown taller since Friday. And more tan. *Which would make sense as he had spent the weekend at the beach, not in boring, hotter-than-hot Palm Springs, visiting relatives like some unfortunate people.* I stared over in his direction, contemplating the misery of my life, and trying to think of some witty and impressive thing to say to him. Which should be easy for me, as the celebrity reporter for *The Hollywoodland Star*, but every time I get within three feet of him, the only language I seem to know is gibberish.

"Mmm, these are good," said Marcy, chomping on my curly fries. My plate was half-empty.

"Hey, how many did you take? How long have you been here?"

"A while," she grinned. "You were preoccupied." She bent her tall body onto the bench and tucked her legs under the table. "Here come Kiki and Luzie."

Luzie bounded over, slid off her iPod headphones and smiled. "I have got to download some of that bagpipe music. It's so dreamy and romantic."

"Yeah, it spoke to me too," agreed Marcy, pressing her nose ring back into place. She glues it on as she's not fully committed yet to her new Goth look. "Lots of angst. I could put some soulful poetry to that. Zack would really like it." She's into this boy in her poetry class. He's like Marcy, clever with words and sensitive, but also a sick skateboarder, always popping ollies and stuff.

"You have got to be kidding," shrieked Kiki, big brown eyes bugging, and earrings jangling in outrage. "It was hideous!"

"Yeah, we should raise money for the 'Rid the planet of bagpipes and do everyone a favor' charity," I said. "Now that would be giving back and feeling good."

Kiki and I roared with laughter and high-fived each other. Then Luzie and Marcy joined in.

It was good to be able to disagree and still all be friends.

"But seriously, what charity should we choose?" I asked. "I have to work my column around it." Usually I just choose to write about whichever celebrity is promoting a new movie or album, or in town for a concert. This was different.

"What about USA Harvest? They pick up food from my dad's restaurant and deliver it to homeless shelters," suggested Luzie.

"Zack's group is doing them," said Marcy. "Anyway, I thought we were going for a charity that helps animals. Seeing as we're raising money by walking dogs."

Kiki grimaced and rolled her eyes, all attitude. "I saw a dog walker with seven dogs this weekend, and she looked so uncool."

Luzie laughed. She has a casual, sporty look—she spends half the week playing varsity soccer for good old Hollywoodland High—and loves to tease Kiki, the fashion Olympian of our group.

"Don't worry, Kiki. You can be a glam dog walker with just two dogs. We wouldn't want to spoil your fashion diva image. Not even for a good cause."

"So, let's find ourselves a charity. And a concerned celebrity for my column," I said.

I pulled my Macbook out of my bag and powered up. "You're so lucky to have computer privileges," said Marcy. I grinned. "Well, as a celebrity reporter you never can tell when you might need to Google. Always prepared. That's my journalistic motto."

All three of my friends groaned in unison. Luzie clamped her iPod headphones onto her ears. I typed in the words CELEBRITY CHARITY DOGS and up popped Jude Law, Scarlett Johansson, and the headline "Selena Gomez feeds homeless dogs." Ooh, this could be good. I clicked on the link and scanned the article. "Did you know that Selena Gomez is a dog lover, and she is helping an organization in Puerto Rico to save homeless dogs in the Caribbean?"

"And," added Marcy, reading over my shoulder, "this gets even better. She's doing an auction this week in Griffith Park, and all proceeds go to the charity. We could donate our money online and win one of the prizes."

"Like a day shopping with Selena. That would be awesome," said Kiki, all excited. "She has great style."

"Or a visit to the set of *Wizards of Waverly Place*," added Luzie. She must know how to lip-read because she never misses a moment of conversation, even with music pounding in her ears.

"I love that show...." I said. I stopped mid-sentence. *My heart plummeted like a rock to the bottom of my stomach.*

"Omigod!" I said. "She was at the beach too, wasn't she?" I wasn't talking about Selena Gomez anymore.

My friends turned and followed my line of vision, just in time to see a tanned Sondra sit down at Jack's table and smile sassily at him. She leaned towards him like she'd known him forever, whispered something, and giggled. Then she must have felt the laser-like glare of eight eyes glowering at her, because she turned, flicked her beach-blond hair, waved at us, and simpered. Like a puppy. But not that cute. Needless to say, we did not return the wave.

"She was, wasn't she?" I asked.

Luzie, Marcy, and Kiki exchanged glances.

"Yeah," said Kiki. "She was there."

"And she's really into Jack," added Marcy, just in case it wasn't obvious enough already.

"But that doesn't mean he likes her," said Luzie. "I mean, Philip Pendleton IV likes you but it doesn't mean that you like him back, does it?" she added brightly.

I gave her a look. "What is there not to like about Sondra? Look at her. She's hot. And so is he.

They're perfect for each other." *I felt like I was nine years old. I wanted to hide under our table and cry.*

"I can't believe you're putting yourself down like that," said Marcy. "You look great too. But you know what...maybe Jack's not that shallow. Maybe he actually likes the fact that you have a brain, and you're funny and smart. Sondra doesn't have anything on you. All she does is shop and flirt."

"Thanks," I said quietly. It was good to have friends, but my stomach still felt as if I'd swallowed a toad. Maybe I could work on my shopping and flirting skills, and I'd be fine. *Maybe.*

I pulled together the last of my courage to look over in Sondra's direction. What if she and Jack were holding hands, or worse, kissing or something? My life would be over. So I was happy to see Sondra eating salad all on her own while Jack, Toby, and Joey made their way across the lunchroom to our table. *Our table?* What were they thinking? Why would they want to be over here? I started to panic inside.

"Hey, Joey," said Luzie, putting her arm around him, and grinning. "Que pasa?" I tried not to stare but I couldn't help it, they were so natural together, so happy with each other. I wondered what it would be like to have a boyfriend.

"Hi, Harlee," said Toby. His hair was very blond. "How come you weren't at the beach this weekend? We could have used you on our volleyball team, right Kiki?"

Kiki giggled. "We sure could."

"Right," I said, "'cos I'm just that good at volleyball." Toby grinned. I grinned back. He was so easy to talk to.

"Maybe this weekend," said Jack. "All of you," he waved his hand in the direction of Kiki and Marcy as well. He looked at me, and my heart stopped.

"Yeah, we'll, we'll…," I started.

"…brush up on our volleyball skills," continued Marcy. "And our speaking skills too." She rolled her eyes and looked in my direction.

As they walked away, I put my head in my hands and moaned. "How can he like me because I'm smart? How can he like me at all? I turn into a weasel from Mars or something whenever he's around. I don't stand a chance against Sondra."

Maybe Sondra heard her name or maybe she'd been staring at us for a long time, but at that point I became aware of her glaring in our general direction.

"Don't sweat it," said Kiki. "Just pretend you're talking to someone else when you're talking to him, someone like…" She scanned the lunchroom. "Like Philip Pendleton IV. Who, by the way, is bearing down on you, Harlee."

I braced myself for the attack.

"Harlee! Who's your column on this week?"

"Selena Gomez," I said. "And I'll need tickets to her charity event on Thursday. Four tickets. Could you swing that?"

A flash of annoyance furrowed Philip's brow. *Just what I needed. Someone else glowering at me, sending bad karma my way.* Then an idea popped into my head, and in that inspirational moment I changed from Harlee Harte, blathering imbecile, into Harlee Harte, queen of smooth-talking. *I could do this.*

"I'd be so grateful if you could, Philip. It'll make the column amazing," I said, with such charm and fluttering of eyelashes that he opened his mouth, said, "Oh, great, what? Sure, no problem. Thanks," quickly closed it and walked off.

Behind me I heard Luzie, Marcy, and Kiki collapse into sniggers of laughter.

"Oh, my. What have we unleashed? Leave that poor boy alone," said Kiki.

That Evening...

"Did you know it costs $30 an hour to have your dog walked in Los Angeles?" asked Luzie. We were at Marcy's house planning our fund-raiser and researching my column. "We're just charging $25 and that includes a cookout in the park afterwards."

"It's so nice of your dad to help out with everything, Luzie," I said looking up from my computer.

"Think how much money we're going to make. I could get that dress I love at BCBG," squealed Kiki.

"Or we could give the money to Selena Gomez's charity auction and help the dogs in the Caribbean," said Marcy with a grin. "Like we're supposed to. When we're done with this, you can become a professional dog walker. You can practice on Chili." On hearing his name, Marcy's dog trotted over to them, tail wagging, tongue out.

"Did you know Selena Gomez adopted a dog from a shelter too?" I said, looking up from my computer. "She has four dogs. Everything I've read about her makes her sound so sweet. I hope we get to meet her."

"Me too," said Marcy. "I'll research her music for you, Harlee. I know her favorite band is Paramore. They're awesome."

"And I'll keep watching *Wizards of Waverly Place*. I love that show," said Luzie in excitement. "Remember the episode with the love potion?" She giggled, her hand over her mouth, in a way that made her look adorable.

"That would be so useful," I blurted out. "I could use it on Jack. Marcy would use it on Zack, and Kiki would... Hey, what about you, Kiki? You've been very quiet about your crushes lately."

"Oh, I don't know," she said. But she looked embarrassed and suddenly seemed very interested in the dog-walking posters we had printed out.

"I think we need a truth spell for Kiki," said Marcy.

The next day...

I love my BFFs. Somehow, by the time I got to school, after a horrifying visit to the dentist, they had signed up 10 dogs for dog-walking. In one hour. And one of them is Buster, Jack Kelly's Jack

Russell. Who knew he even had a dog? But there was his name on the list, signed by his own hand in the very pen I was now holding. I counted up those dogs—Mr. Thomas's dog, Brownie; Philip's dog, Amber; Marcy's Chili; and seven others all set and ready for walking. Ten at $25 each...so we had raised $250 for Selena's charity. It was awesome. And if we were walking Jack's dog then that meant that he would be at the cookout tomorrow too.

"He asked where you were, Harlee," said Luzie.

I grinned and whooped. "Could life get any better?"

That's when Kiki opened her Juicy Couture bag to show me four tickets. "Philip stopped by with these. For tomorrow's auction," she said.

Wow. Amazing what a little flirting can do.

Later that week...

Okay, so maybe squeezing four girls and ten dogs into the back of a van was not a good idea, but it was our best option for getting out to Griffith Park on time and all together. Luzie's dad, Carlos, looked over his shoulder every couple of minutes, slapped his thigh and roared with laughter, then turned his attention back to the highway. "I am happy today is my day off," he must have said a million times, as he grinned that same smile that Luzie has.

"My clothes are ruined!" Kiki said miserably. "I've been trampled alive."

"Lucky we brought a change of clothing for the auction," I said as Buster bounded across me and hurdled into the front seat. "Hola!" shouted Carlos in surprise. Next thing we knew Buster was standing with his front paws on the back of the seat with a string of sausages in his mouth. "Those are for the cookout!" yelled Luzie. But Buster just shook his head.

"Lucky we have plenty more!" laughed Carlos.

Later...

"This reminds me of when I was little," said Kiki. "We used to come to the carousel here all the time."

"Me too," I said. "But I loved the pony rides the best."

"We still come here with Chili," said Marcy. "I'll show you his favorite trail." So we said good-bye to Carlos at the picnicking site with a promise of being back there in an hour and a half. The air smelled so clean and fresh as we walked along a tree-lined trail, and I was thinking about how we should do this more often, get out into nature, when I narrowly missed stepping into a big patch of horse manure. *Nice.*

The dogs all trotted along on their leashes. I had Buster, of course, and Bella, a golden lab who belonged to Toby's neighbor. We were pretty good, I thought, for nonprofessional dog-walkers. We gave the dogs water from plastic bowls we had brought along and scooped up their poop into plastic bags. About an hour into our walk we sat down in the shade of some ancient trees, drank diet Cokes, and gave the dogs biscuits. They all gnawed happily except for Mr. Thomas's dog, Brownie, who growled at me when my cell phone rang, which made perfect sense, considering how Mr. Thomas has a huge issue with cell phones in class.

"We should go," said Luzie, looking at her watch. "Otherwise my dad will worry." He didn't seem like the worrying type, but we set off anyway. And I don't know if there was caffeine or sugar in those dog biscuits, but Buster started running around like crazy, bounding ahead of me as far as his leash would take him, while Bella sniffed at the trunk of every tree until I was pulled from one to the other, and my arms felt like they were about to drop off.

"My dogs are incompatible," I announced. "They are exact opposites. Can I switch?"

"You could take Lulu. She's active," said Kiki. She happily handed over the little Maltese, and I sped off after my two energetic pups. Looking back over my shoulder, I noticed Kiki strolling along as Bella, Amber, and Brownie puttered around her in the sunlight. I pulled hard on my leashes, and that brought my dogs up sharp. They stopped, looked at me with puzzled expressions, then completely ignored me and raced off again.

"Harlee! Wait up!" It was Marcy. She caught up with me with long sprinter strides. "You have to let them know who is boss, or they'll drag you all the way back home. Like this." She took Buster's leash and gave it a gentle, but definite, tug. "Buster, stop." Buster stopped.

"Buster, sit." Buster sat. Then he rolled in the grass and lay down for his tummy to be rubbed.

"You're good," I said. "You try," said Marcy.

She handed over the leash. I took it, gave a gentle, but definite, tug. Buster looked at me over his shoulder. With a mischievous look in his eyes he ran even faster. I tugged again, but he took off again. And this time the leash slipped off my hand, fell into the grass, and followed Buster across the field.

"He got loose! He's running away." All I could see was Jack Kelly's dog vanishing into the trees ahead of me. I started running, dragging Lulu with me.

Behind me, I heard Marcy yell, "Buster's escaped," and she, Kiki, and Luzie hurtled after me.

"Buster!" I screamed. "Buster!" But there was no sign of the little Jack Russell.

We all stood together in the trees, sweaty and muddy, and definitely not looking our best. I had lost Jack's dog. Not only was I a bumbling bobble-head and not as gorgeous as Sondra, but I had now officially lost his dog. There was no hope for me. *I may as well just hike straight into the woods and live on wild onions and mushrooms and never be seen again because there was no way that I was going to be able to look Jack in the face ever again.* Tears started down my face, and the only happy thought in my mind right then was that I had been smart enough to wear waterproof mascara that morning.

"We have to go back," said Luzie. "Or my dad will send out a search party. Buster will turn up, Harlee. Dogs always do."

I shook my head. "I have to find him, even if I stay here all night."

"I'll stay with her," said Kiki. "You two go back to your dad. We'll stay on the trail where it's safe, and we have our phones. We'll keep my three dogs, but Lulu goes back with you."

I could have hugged her. She was so together. I should have known that cool, chic Kiki would be calm in an emergency.

So Kiki and I stayed and yelled for that pesky dog until our voices were hoarse and our deodorant went into overdrive. But he did not show up. We left dog biscuits on rocks and used Brownie, Amber, and Bella as tracker dogs, but they were useless and just wanted to lie down in the shade. Which is exactly what Kiki and I wanted to do but we didn't.

We sent out pleading wishes and made all kinds of promises to ourselves—"if Buster shows up safe and sound I'll do chores without complaining for a month," "I'll be nice to my little brother, Alec," "I'll join a gym." But that little dog did not show up.

"Harlee! Kiki!" Someone was yelling our names, coming back up the trail. We turned, and to my horror, I saw Jack and Toby hiking towards us. I wanted to run away or just hide behind Kiki and pretend I was somewhere else. But then I saw that Jack was holding a leash, and on the very end of that leash was Buster.

I rushed up to them, and without even thinking about what I was doing I gave Jack and Buster and Toby some kind of group hug. And then I was babbling. "I'm so sorry," I said. "Where did you find him? He just ran off. I'm the worst dog walker in the whole of LA. We thought he was gone forever, and I was just going to live in the hills and never come home."

To my surprise Jack and Toby and Kiki roared with laughter, and I stopped my torrent of words.

"Well, you can come home now," said Jack. "Buster must have smelled the sausages because we found him back at the picnic area with Carlos— having the time of his life." Then he smiled at me in such a way that I would have blushed bright red except my face was so flushed and sunburnt already that it probably didn't show. I smiled and became speechless again. And as I did, I noticed Kiki smiling at Toby.

"That was nice of you to stay with the mad mountain woman and three dogs," said Toby.

"Well, somebody had to take charge around here," shrugged Kiki. Toby smiled.

"So, how about I help you with those dogs, and we leave Harlee to fend for herself now?" They walked off down the hiking trail leaving Jack and me and Buster to follow.

I didn't care if Sondra were at the cookout looking fresh-as-a-daisy fab. For now I was happy to let my shoulder brush against Jack's and walk in silence with him down the trail to join the others.

Later…

As we walked across to our chairs set out in the grass, I looked at my friends and felt good. We had scrubbed up pretty clean in the back of Carlos's van, and I was happy that Selena's auction was a low-key affair for a bunch of dog-lovers. We had followed her casual sense of style for our clothes, and all of us wore jeans and different layered tops, splashed here and there with bright colors and funky jewelry. We had Chili with us, having returned the other dogs back to their owners at the cookout. I was not holding the leash. I don't think I would hold a dog leash for a long time.

We made it just in time. As we settled into our seats, Selena came onstage and sang "Cruella de Vil" from *101 Dalmatians*. She has a great voice and lots of energy, and so much stage-presence for someone who's the same age as us. I thought to myself that if she wasn't home-schooled then she might have gone to school at Hollywoodland High.

The auction was fun, but I felt bad for Kiki when I saw her look of disappointment that we didn't win the shopping spree. Or the visit to the set of *Wizards*.

"It's OK," whispered Luzie when I squeezed her shoulder. "We still helped the dogs." But then Selena was making an announcement that drew our attention back to her. "Winner of lot number 22, a pair of my favorite Converse sneakers, signed by me, goes to...Harlee Harte!"

I looked at my friends in confusion. *We hadn't bid on this lot, had we?* They looked just as confused as I did.

When the auction was over, a security guard came up to me, "Miss Harte and friends? Selena is waiting for you over here." He led us into a small tent. "You can bring the dog in."

"Harlee, thank you for coming today and for giving money to the auction," Selena said. She smiled and fussed over Chili as I introduced her to Kiki, Marcy, and Luzie.

"And you won these." She handed over the sneakers. "But we didn't bid on those," said Kiki. "We only wanted to win something we could all do together."

Selena stopped for a moment, then consulted a sheet of paper on a clipboard. "You're right. Somebody else bid on them, but they're definitely for Harlee."

"Who?" asked Luzie excitedly.

Selena smiled an impish grin. "I can't really say," she said. "Maybe somebody who likes you?" Smiles broke out on my friends' faces as I blushed.

Then the security guard stuck his head around the door and asked, "Ready?" Selena nodded. "I have to go," she said. "It was great meeting you all. I like the fact that you're such good friends to each other. Friends are really important."

She gave us each a hug then disappeared through a side door.

And I was left holding the shoes and wondering...

At the library...

As I waited for my column to print, I thought about how "Giving Back and Feeling Good" week had turned out to be great. I had worked with my BFFs to give money to a good cause and had had a blast doing so. I had made Jack laugh—in a good way. *Maybe I would see him at the beach this weekend.* My column was pretty amazing too, at least I thought so.

I pulled it out of the printer and started to read it through.

"I'll take that when you're done," said a bossy voice. Philip Pendleton IV. It struck me then that usually Toby was around when I printed my column, and I wondered where he was.

I handed the paper over. "Thanks," said Philip brusquely as he stuffed it in his messenger bag. I gathered up my stuff and started to walk out of the library, happy to have met my deadline.

"By the way, Harlee," Philip called after me, looking at my new Converse. "Nice shoes."

PART TWO
The Column

THE HOLLYWOODLAND ST★R

VOL. 11 ISSUE 3   HOLLYWOOD, CA

Selena's BD:
July 22, 1992

Selena's Sign:
CANCER
June 22–July 23

Element: Water

Ruling Planet:
The Moon

Symbol:
The Crab

Stone:
Moonstone

Life Pursuit:
Constant
reassurance &
intimacy

Vibration:
Moody

Secret Desire:
To feel safe

HARTEBEAT

by Harlee Harte

I ♡ Selena Gomez.

You all know Selena Gomez as Alex Russo cooking up magic and mischief in the hot TV show *Wizards of Waverly Place*, but I found out this week that she's pretty magical in the real world too. This week's column is dedicated to Selena, and watch out all you wizards-in-training out there, because as you read my column she'll cast her spell over you too. Read on!

Traits:
Compassionate
about friends
and family

Clever and
clear-headed

Hard-working

Like home-
time

Believe in
themselves

Female Celeb
Cancers:
Liv Tyler
Lindsay Lohan
Jessica Simpson

On July 22, 1992, Selena Marie Gomez was born in New York City to parents Ricardo and Mandy. Ricardo was of Mexican descent and Mandy of Italian, and Selena was born with beautiful dark eyes and dark hair. Her father named her Selena, after the Mexican-American singer, Selena Quintanilla Perez. Perhaps he knew that his little Selena would grow up to be a singer too.

Check it out!

Selena Quintanilla-Perez sang a kind of pop-folk music known as tejano. She recorded 9 albums with her band, only 1 in English. She was murdered in 1995 by the president of her fan club, but she is not forgotten. Many fans make the pilgrimage each year to Corpus Christi, Texas, to visit her grave. Selena Gomez was taken there by her dad when she was little and has since met members of the late singer's family.

Soon after she was born, Selena's family moved away from New York City and settled in Texas where both her parents were from, and she would grow up in Grand Prairie, not far from Dallas. She settled happily into her new neighborhood, playing outside with the neighborhood kids, and having plenty of fun. Unfortunately, a little while after their move, her parents divorced. Selena stayed with her mom, Mandy. Later Mandy would marry again, and now Selena lives with her mom and her step-dad, Brian.

In New York Mandy had been involved in the theater community, in both acting and stage makeup, and when Selena was in elementary school in Texas her mom started acting again. Selena has said that she grew up around acting, and by the time she was six she knew that she wanted to have a go at it herself. So her mom took her to her very first audition: an open audition for the television show, *Barney and Friends*.

There were over 1000 kids at the auditions at The Studios in Las Colinas, Texas, all hoping to be cast as regulars on the hit TV show and to star alongside Barney, the famous purple dinosaur. Selena was one of those hopeful children with no prior acting experience just waiting for a chance to impress the casting directors. Standing next to her in the line that day was another little girl, six-year-old Demi Lovato, and when she spread her coat on the ground and asked Selena if she'd like to color in her coloring book with her, it was the start of a long and special friendship. When the girls finally reached the front of the long line of kids and parents, they both did really great auditions. Both girls were invited for callbacks and were both hired for the *Barney* show. They still remain the best of friends today.

On *Barney and Friends* Selena played the role of Gianna and had a great time—and learned a huge amount about the process of acting. She had to learn to work in front of a camera, how to sing and dance, how to memorize lines, and work with other actors. Selena was often picked for funny scenes and learned how to fine tune her sense of comedy and comic timing. The show also taught her how to handle other parts of her life. As she missed chunks of school at a time for filming she needed to work out how to juggle acting and school work. She also had to deal with meanness from some of the kids at school. There were those who taunted her for being on the Barney show, and those who were jealous of her success. In an interview with *Discovery Girls* she said, "I did lose a couple of friends because of the jealousy thing. But I look at it like a sport. Some kids play soccer. Acting is my sport."

She was also lucky to have her mother's support and common-sense advice. After all, her mom had worked in the business and knew enough to help her young daughter through the hard times. She encouraged her to spend time with her family and her friends, the ones who would always be there for her through thick and thin. She also helped her to have a normal childhood, one filled with hanging out at the skate park or the mall or movie theater. Selena has always gravitated towards the down-to-earth, no-nonsense friendships that boys can offer and that has helped to keep her grounded. And she had her best friend, Demi, on the *Barney* set, as her constant companion. Off the set they were able to be friends too as they lived fairly close to each other and were able to have sleepovers at each other's houses. As their acting talent grew so did their friendship.

Selena stayed on the *Barney* show for two seasons and enjoyed her time there. However, she wanted to branch out and develop her acting talents so she looked for other auditions. She also took acting and singing lessons, and these paid off as she was offered several parts in TV commercials. Next she landed a small role in a feature film, *Spy Kids 3*, where she played the part of a girl in a water park. It was not a big part, but every piece of work was valuable as it taught Selena more and more about the acting world, and her name was becoming known to casting directors and agents. She was still only eleven years old.

Her next step forward was getting a part in Walker, *Texas Ranger: Trial by Fire*. It was a made-for-television movie special of the popular TV series with Chuck Norris. Selena was thrilled to play a part in this popular show set in her home state.

Next, Selena was booked as one of the lead characters in a pilot for a children's television show called *Brain Zapped*. A television pilot is a test episode of an intended television series. It's like a sample show that television networks look at and analyze to decide whether they want to go ahead with the expense of a whole television series based on the pilot. Selena was cast as book-lover Emily Grace Garcia, who investigates strange goings-on at the local library—the building seems to look alive. Things get even more bizarre when Emily and her friend, Kingston, witness electric holograms shooting out of books and find themselves thrust into another world.

As Selena sings in the theme song, "My mom always told me books could take you into a whole new world, but. . . I don't think this is what she meant." This acting experience would be Selena's first introduction to the green screen which would be helpful to her later on. She and her co-star did most of their work in an all-green room so that during editing the green background could be replaced with another—more interesting— background. In this way, it seemed, in the final version of the show, as if Selena had traveled back to prehistoric times and was hanging out with dinosaurs. Those clever special effects! Unfortunately for Selena—and all who worked on *Brain Zapped*—the pilot wasn't picked up by television networks and so didn't become the series they had hoped for. Selena was disappointed and had to learn the hard lesson that not everything works out the way you want it to. It wouldn't be the only time she had to deal with disappointment.

Many people give up when life lets them down, but Selena didn't, and with the support of her mother, she set off on a four-hour car drive to Austin, Texas, for an open-casting call for the Disney Channel. It was a similar experience to her first-ever audition: thousands of hopefuls looking for that one-shot opportunity to impress. Except there were differences too. Selena was no longer a seven-year-old who thinks she'd like to give acting a go. Now she really knew that this was what she wanted for herself, and she wanted it body and soul. She had worked very hard for the last five years at her acting, dancing and singing and so, for her, the stakes were very much higher now. Despite her nerves, Selena's audition went well. It went so well in fact, that she was invited out to Los Angeles to audition for Disney executives. Again, her audition was impressive, and she caught the eye of Gary Marsh, the president of entertainment for Disney Channel Worldwide. In an interview with

EW.com he said her audition was "green, it was rough—but she had that It factor."

As a result of her auditions, Selena was offered a role in a pilot for a television series. She was excited to play the role of Stevie Sanchez in *What's Stevie Thinking?* alongside Lalaine Vergara-Paras from the popular Disney show *Lizzie McGuire*. Lalaine played Lizzie McGuire's best friend, Miranda Sanchez, on the show, and this new show would follow Miranda and her little sister, Stevie (played by Selena). Selena had always been a big fan of *Lizzie McGuire*, and so it was fun for her to take on the role and be related to that show. She was also pleased that this would be the first Disney show to star a Hispanic family.

After the initial excitement of getting the role and becoming part of the Disney family, and then the rewarding work of filming the show, Selena was about to face disappointment again. The pilot was shown to test audiences, and the response was underwhelming. The series was not picked up.

Selena was really beginning to appreciate the ups-and-downs of the acting world. This time it was a little easier for her, however, as she had the knowledge that she had been spotted by Disney—and hopefully there would be more work coming to her.

There was. She was offered two new roles in pilots, and she happily accepted them—even if they might end in disappointment again. She knew that the price of success can often be failure but she was willing to try again—and again— for her dream of acting.

The first pilot she worked on was a spinoff of the popular show, *The Suite Life of Zack and Cody*, with the twins, Cole and Dylan Sprouse. The lead character was Arwin, engineer of the Tipton Hotel, and Selena played Chloe, one of his nieces. Once again this show did not test as well as expected with test audiences and went no further.

The second show, however, was a pilot called *Wizards of Waverly Place*. When Selena auditioned for the role of Alex Russo, she went in and presented her version of Alex. She told the *OC Register* that Alex is "very spunky. I didn't want her to be a kind of girly girl. So she's the Converse-wearing, outgoing one, always getting in trouble and getting her brothers in trouble as well." The producers loved her version. But how would test audiences react to Alex and the rest of the Russo family? Luckily, this series about a family of teenage wizards living in New York City tested very well and became a popular series. At last one of Selena's television show pilots was green-lit, and Selena would star in a TV series! Her hard work had paid off.

When Selena received the telephone call from Los Angeles to Texas telling her that *Wizards of Waverly Place* was a go and that she was to be signed up for the first season, it was huge and exciting news. Her life was about to change. And not just her life, but that of her whole family. For her other television work, Selena had been able to live in Texas and travel back and forth but now that she had steady work on a series she would have to move to Los Angeles. And, as she was still young, her family would have to move with her. This was a big commitment for her mom and her step-dad as they had jobs and friends and a house in Texas. But they agreed to it, and so Selena and her mom moved out first, while Brian stayed behind with the four dogs to close things up in Texas. Disney was very helpful in relocating their new young star and provided financial help to make the move possible, and Selena's mom has always been grateful for that.

This is what Selena told *Tiger Beat* magazine about her family: "My mom and step-dad are my two biggest supporters. But they also keep me very grounded. You still have to do your chores."

LA or BUST!

Quickly after moving into a big loft in downtown LA, Selena was working hard again. She was cast as a guest star on two enormously popular

Disney shows: *Hannah Montana* and *The Suite Life of Zack and Cody*. The idea was to introduce her to Disney fans before her own show made its appearance, and this was a good way to do it. Her first guest role was in an episode of *The Suite Life* called "A Midsummer's Nightmare," and she played Gwen, Cody's love interest. However, when Gwen is cast in the school play and has to kiss Cody's brother, Zack, all sorts of funny problems arise. Selena had a blast in the filming of this episode and even managed her first on-screen kiss.

Her second guest role was on *Hannah Montana* where she played the mean character, Mikayla, who is determined to steal all Hannah's fans. It was her first mean-girl role, and she played it so well and so convincingly that she was invited back for several more episodes. She and Miley Cyrus, the star of the show, became friends during filming. But Selena did not forget her old friend, Demi, and wished that she could be out in LA with her, acting or singing too. She was able to make that wish come true by letting Demi know about a casting for a new Disney series, *As the Bell Rings*, a short television series. After some tough auditions, Selena was excited to hear that her friend had earned herself a part. It is especially nice that Selena was able to reach out to her friend in such a competitive world where many people think only of themselves and how to get ahead. Probably Selena knew that Demi would have done the same for her.

Finally it was time for Selena to start filming *Wizards of Waverly Place*. She had worked hard and waited for a long time for this break, and she was ready to give her best performance. She plays the part of Alex Russo, a modern-day wizard. She is the middle child and only girl, and both her brothers (Justin, played by David Henrie and Max, played by Jake T. Austin) have magical powers too. Once they are adults only one of the three children will be able to keep their magical gift—the one who wins a special magic competition. Their father, Jerry, won his family's competition, but he gave up his powers to marry a mortal, their mother, and so his powers passed on to his brother, the children's uncle. Even though the children are not supposed to use their magic while unsupervised, they often do, and Alex, especially, ends up getting into a lot of trouble. Then she uses her magic to get herself out of trouble—with some very funny results.

Check it out!

If Selena could choose a magical skill, she would like to be able to duplicate herself so that she could skip class.

Selena loves playing the character of Alex as in some ways she is very like her—her sporty, no-nonsense attitude and her ability to have fun. However, Selena doesn't usually get into quite so much trouble. She told PBSKids of the similarities between her and Alex: "I'm outgoing just like Alex is, but she gets into a lot of trouble, and I don't get into trouble like she does, that's for sure. I guess style-wise, we're kind of similar. I like to dress very relaxed, and Alex just wears Converse and jeans and cute tops, and that's me, too." She especially liked the fact that the show's producers and writers were interested in how she viewed her character and went with her ideas on how to keep her "edgy" and not a "girly girl."

Interestingly enough, the aspects of the show that Selena likes best are not the most obvious ones. Sure she likes to play sassy, down-to-earth Alex with her Converse sneakers and destined-for-trouble ways. She also loves the special effects that come with a show with magical elements and with them one never really knows what's going to happen on a day of filming. But it is the family scenes that have made the most impression on her. She told PBSKids, "Whether it's a funny or dramatic scene, whether we're trying to solve a problem or doing magic or turning my brother invisible, it comes off best when we're with the whole family in the loft. I think that when we're all together the show is at its strongest point. And I love being with the entire cast in a scene." This could be because Selena is so close to her family and understands the real importance of a supportive family in one's life.

Selena's favorite shoes are Converse sneakers. She owns over 20 pairs, and it was her idea to have her *Wizards of Waverly Place* character, Alex, wear Converse too!

It is also clear that Selena enjoys being on the first Disney series featuring a Hispanic family (that made it beyond a pilot). She told BlogAMole, "I think that makes me feel so proud of where I come from because I do feel like it's a huge step for the Disney channel to have their first Latin show. It's incredible and I am happy to be a part of that family." Her mom on the show, Theresa Russo (played by Maria Canals-Barrera), is Mexican and teaches the Russo family the importance of their heritage, and the show presents the Russos as a mix of Mexican and Italian (just like Selena herself!) and highlights different aspects of these cultures. It reminds her of ways in which her own family keeps its traditions alive. She continued in her interview with BlogAMole, "When I go back home, we do the same things that we always do. There is this park right in front of my grandma's house and believe it or not I have eighty cousins! So we all get together as a family and my grandma makes her rice, my other abuelita makes her soup, and my aunt makes her tamales. That is our moment to be together."

♡ Selena's Latin Roots ♡

In Latin American culture the **Quinceanera** is a coming-of-age celebration that takes place on (or around) a girl's fifteenth birthday. While Selena was not able to have this special celebration because she was working, her character on *Wizards of Waverly Place* does celebrate when she turns fifteen.

Selena is proud of her Mexican-Italian heritage and joined up with MisQuinceMag.com, a Web site designed for planning quinceaneras. Their motto is "Dream for 15," encouraging girls to dream big for their fifteenth birthday but to dream even bigger for the next fifteen years of their life to make their lifelong dreams come true.

When asked by MisQuinceMag.com to be a part of this campaign Selena was happy to join the cause and reach out to Latina girls in the online community. She designed a cute tee shirt with butterflies and the words "Dream Out loud," "Love always," and "Believe in yourself."

Proceeds from the shirt went to the Palomita Education Fund that helps send under-privileged Latinos to college.

Selena has said that when she was younger and went along to auditions that she wished she looked like all the blond-haired, blue-eyed girls who were also auditioning. But as she grew older she learned to appreciate her look. She told *Twist* magazine: "I don't know if I would've had the opportunity to be on *Wizards of Waverly Place* if it weren't for my heritage." In an interview with *Latina* magazine she said, "One day being with my dad, it hit me: it's pretty neat to be Mexican. And there aren't enough Latinas in Hollywood—or there are, but they don't get the recognition. So to be able to come out here and use that, it's really a powerful thing." It makes her feel proud of who she is and where she comes from when moms come up to her after a show or a taping and say, "It's so wonderful to see a Latina that my kids can look up to."

The cast of *Wizards of Waverly Place* is incredibly close, and the three siblings and Alex's best friend, Harper (played by Jennifer Stone), spend a lot of time together both on and off the set.

Selena grew up as an only child, and she feels that she has now learned what it is like to have siblings—and she loves it! She refers to David Henrie and Jake T. Austin as her "real brothers." They are very protective of her. She says that they all hang out together when they are not filming and love to go to the beach to go surfing on the weekend. They also go to the movies and sing karaoke together—just like regular siblings. And sometimes they even fight. Their off-screen friendship has definitely helped them to bond on set and has brought a higher level of chemistry to their performances.

Of course, Selena learned a huge amount over the course of filming the first season, and one thing that was especially helpful to her was to see how the live audiences would react to some of the comic scenes that had been worked on earlier in the week. She has said that she is really grateful to the people who come and see the lived tapings as she loves performing to an audience. She also realized during those tapings that she was beginning to get fans. It was a surprise to her, and a little strange at first as she realized that she was just as nervous and excited about meeting fans as they were about meeting her.

Selena had very busy days when working on the filming of the series because not only did she have to memorize her lines, and rehearse over and over before the final taping of each show, she also had schoolwork to do. Selena, Jen, and Jake all had to work with tutors each day to make sure that they were on top of their work, and only after it was all finished were they allowed to have free time. Selena liked to play basketball on the on-set court and even managed to beat her twelve-year-old "real brother" Jake sometimes.

On October 12, 2007, the first episode of *Wizards of Waverly Place* premiered on the Disney Channel. Almost 6 million people watched the first episode, and the show soon gained itself loyal fans. They liked the combination of magic and humor but also the real-life teenage problems that the

Russo siblings handled. They especially loved Selena as Alex Gomez—she was cool. As more and more viewers watched the show each week Disney announced that they would sign up the cast for a second season. They also announced a one hour-long television special in which Alex and Justin go to summer school at Wiz Tech, and Selena dresses up in a Harry Potter-type black gown and big glasses! This special aired in April 2008 and had a record number of viewers.

Almost overnight Selena became a star, and with this new role would come a lot of pressure. She would begin to be recognized in public and have her life scrutinized by the media. Photographs would appear of her and rumors would abound. Was she ready to handle the fame? Peter Murrieta, executive producer of *Wizards of Waverly Place*, told the *OC Register*: "It's very difficult to be a teenager, period. Without anything else, it's just a hard thing. When you add the possibility of becoming a star almost exactly overnight, it just makes it more stressful. What I can say about both Selena and Jennifer (Stone) is that they are great people who have their heads on their shoulders right." This is something that is said over and over about Selena: she has her head on her shoulders and her feet on the ground. Is she ever going to let fame go to her head and turn into a wild celebrity? Probably not. She told *TV Guide*, "To be honest, I'm quite boring! I love to go bowling and to the movies." And, of course, if she ever forgets who she really is, she can rely on her mother to remind her. She told *Extra*, "My mom's there to say, 'The moment I see you get big headed or changing, I will drag you right back home to Texas and we are moving away from here.'"

Selena was able to use one of her other talents on *Wizards of Waverly Place*—her singing. She recorded the theme tune for the series, *Everything Is Not What It Seems*, and her voice together with the song's lyrics seems to perfectly fit the tone of the series.

Selena was lucky enough to be able to pursue other acting work as *Wizards of Waverly Place* takes several months off from filming each year. Obviously, now that she is the star of a hit television show and has a strong fan base, many offers of work have come Selena's way. But she doesn't accept every role. She has to think about what she likes, what her goals are, and what she wants the future to hold. When she was offered a role in *High School Musical 3* she turned it down, even though it was sure to be a commercial success and would have gained her more media exposure.

"*High School Musical 3* is cute, and I think it would be a great opportunity for someone else," Selena told the *New York Daily News*. "But I passed on it because I didn't want to do it. I plan to take other roles in acting that are challenging for me. After Disney, I want to be taken seriously as an actress for many years."

The next project that she signed up for was a voice-over role in the animated version of the Dr. Seuss classic, *Horton Hears a Who*. She had never tried animation before and told the *New York Daily*

News it would be "cool to try something different." It would certainly be a way of challenging herself and expanding her horizons. The movie took the book's original premise and expanded on it, following the story of Horton (an elephant) who discovers a microscopic world of tiny creatures called Whos and takes upon himself the role of their protector. Selena provided the voices for the daughters of the Mayor of Whoville—there were ninety of them, and all were called Helga! I voiced all of them," continued Selena. "I had to change up my voice to do higher voices, and then bring it down to do lower voices. All of the Mayor's daughters look different, so I play many different characters." The Mayor of Whoville himself was played by Steve Carell, and Selena had been excited at the prospect of meeting him and some of the other stars of the film (including Jim Carrey). But, as it turned out, they recorded their parts separately, and she never got to meet him. One day she hopes that she will, and then she'll be able to say, "Hey, I played your daughter!" All ninety of them!

Working on *Horton Hears a Who* was a great experience for Selena as she learned many new things. She also loved watching a favorite childhood book being brought to life on the big screen. She has said that she was a huge fan of Dr. Seuss when growing up. "I remember reading his books like crazy with my grandmother when I was younger." (*New York Daily News*)

Selena's next project was pure Disney as she took on the movie role of a modern-day Cinderella. And even if Selena wasn't really into dress-up and princesses when she was growing up, the new take on Cinderella—a girl who follows her dreams to become a dancer—must have appealed immensely to Selena and felt especially close to her heart as she has followed her acting dreams her whole life. *Another Cinderella Story* tells the tale of a girl called Mary Santiago who lives with an unpleasant former pop star, Dominique, and her two mean daughters,

Britt and Bree. Mary is an amazing hip-hop and tango dancer and dreams to go to the Manhattan School of Dance on a scholarship. She catches the eye of pop star JP at a school masked ball. They dance together but before they can connect Mary must run home. In true modern Cinderella style she drops her MP3 player leaving him with just one clue as to her identity: her four most played tunes. Later, to win over Mary and prove his love to her, JP holds a dance competition for his new music video.

At last, all those hours of singing and dancing lessons paid off for Selena in this high-energy musical. She got to sing three songs in the movie: "Tell Me Something I Don't Know," "Bang a Drum," and "New Classic" (sung with co-star Drew Seeley who was Zac Efron's voice in *High School Musical*). There was also plenty of dancing. Selena found some of the dance numbers difficult to master but she enjoyed the challenge. She even took tango lessons and told MTV, "My favorite musical number has to be the tango piece," she said. "It's when the two characters meet and fall in love. It's one of the hardest dances I've learned, but the most beautiful." When Selena was growing up in Texas, one of the things she loved to do was hang out at skate parks. Her skate-boarding moves were needed for this movie as her character, Mary, was forced to skate board home from school each day while the nasty Britt and Bree got to ride in the limo!

Another Cinderella Story was originally planned to premiere in April 2008, but in the end it was released straight to DVD instead. It was said to be a financial decision. Again, Selena faced the disappointment of things not going according to plan, but she was excited to have taken on the role, was pleased with her performance, and accepted the reality of the decision. There would be plenty of time for other big-screen performances. After all she was still very young!

The year 2008 would be huge for Selena. Not only was it the year of *Horton Hears A Who* and *Another Cinderella Story*, it was also the year that she was signed up by a record label, Hollywood Records. Ever since her *Barney* days, Selena has loved to sing, and now she will have a chance to work on her own album. Selena told MTV, "I'm going to be in a band. I basically want to make music that…parents and kids can jump around to and have a good time." She has said that her idea of the perfect band "would have all guys in it." Apparently the Jonas Brothers have been helping her through the recording process. Her album will have a pop/rock feel, and she'll be singing and playing a few instruments as well. She has been learning to play the drums—and has been seen around town with her drumsticks—and also the electric guitar. This is what she told PBSKids about the difference between singing and acting: "I think you can be more of yourself when you're singing. You can have a little bit more control over it. It's a different process, with going into the studio and not having to worry about what you look like on camera. You write music and perform it, have fun,

SELENA'S PLAYLIST

PARAMORE

This pop-rock band from Tennessee is Selena's favorite band. She admires lead singer, Hayley Williams, and would love to collaborate with the band one day.

FOREVER THE SICKEST KIDS

This is an all-male rock band from Selena's home-state of Texas. Selena has jammed with them and they have joined her in the studio to help come up with new material for her album.

THE JONAS BROTHERS

Selena is good friends with all three brothers having met them through Demi Lovato when she starred in *Camp Rock* with them. Selena appeared in the music video for their single "Burnin' Up."

TAYLOR SWIFT

Selena and Taylor are very close friends. Taylor's *Fearless* is one of Selena's favorite songs, and she has said they have talked about writing a song together.

then go on concert and jam out in front of an audience." She makes it all sound so easy.

Another of Selena's singing projects was released at about this time, the song *Fly to Your Heart* from the soundtrack of the animated movie, *Tinkerbell*.

When Selena's next project was decided, it brought with it some exciting news for the young actress. For the first time since *Barney and Friends*, Selena would be working with her best friend, Demi Lovato. The two girls

DEMI LOVATO
Selena's BFF is one of her favorite singers too.

**HANNAH MONTANA/
MILEY CYRUS**
The fun, bouncy "Rock Star" is one of Selena's fave songs to sing and dance around to.

FALL OUT BOY
a punk pop band or emo group from Illinois. The band consists of Patrick Stump (vocals and guitar), Joe Trohman (guitar and vocals), Pete Wentz (bass guitar and vocals), and Andy Hurley (drums and percussion).

must have been thrilled! They were cast for an original made-for-television movie, *Princess Protection Program*. Only one of them gets to play a princess—and this time it is not Selena. Instead she won the role of Carter Mason, a tomboy, whose father heads up a secretive organization, the Princess Protection Agency. He is charged with protecting Princess Rosalinda of Costa Luna in South America when she has to flee for her life after an evil dictator, General Kane, takes over her country. The idea is that Rosalinda will move in with the Masons, pretending to be a cousin, and Carter will help "Rosie" to adjust to life as an ordinary American teenager. Things, of course, do not always go according to plan, especially as Princess Rosalinda has difficulties leaving her royal habits behind. And when Carter's crush begins to fall for Rosie some awkward situations arise. It must have been interesting for Selena and Demi to play rivals instead of best friends!

Filming took place in Puerto Rico, and the two friends were able to spend a lot of time together, staying in the same hotel, rehearsing together, and getting schoolwork done. The girls were also able to sing together as the movie features a duet called "One and the Same" to which they recorded a music video too. A track from Demi's debut album *Don't Forget* will also be in the movie.

Check it out!

Selena and BFF Demi Lovato have matching pink guitar-pick necklaces.

It is a song called "Two Worlds Collide," and originally Demi wrote it for her best friend Selena.

The two friends would get another chance quite quickly to work together again, this time in a television series, starring Demi in one of the lead roles, *Sonny with a Chance*. Demi plays a girl from the midwest who is chosen to star in a television series and must move to Los Angeles (sound familiar?). So far Selena has been invited to appear as a guest star in some of the episodes.

Selena on the move!

The next exciting news for Selena was that there would be a movie version of *Wizards of Waverly Place* to air on the Disney Channel. She would get to spend time with some of her favorite people on the beautiful island of Puerto Rico—again! She wrote on her MySpace page, "Puerto Rico is honestly one of the most beautiful places in the world. The sweetest people and energy. I suggest to everyone to run away here one day. It will make you a better person.... Thank you Puerto Rico." Then she would come back to shoot the rest of the movie in New York. Her schedule could not get much fuller. The only thing that could make Selena a little unhappy with all the great things that were happening to her in her career could be that she is away from Texas so much, and that she misses her family. She told the *LA Times*, "I'm from Texas, and I don't get to go home often. I miss the normality and also that it's not so populated. I'm from a small town, and I still love going home and being able to drive at 7 in the morning and there not be any traffic. And I miss my family. They're the reason I am the person I am today."

And it seems that Selena may not be heading home anytime soon as she received some more exciting news: she heard that her acting repertoire would be expanding even further. She has been cast in a movie adaptation of Beverly Cleary's popular *Ramona and Beezus*, the first book in the classic series. She will play the part of Beezus/Beatrice Quimby, bossy older sister to the exasperating Ramona. It will be a great role for Selena, and a nice way to make a feature film debut. Elizabeth Allen, who directed *Aquamarine* (the mermaid movie) will direct. It will be interesting for Selena to experience having a little sister, especially one like Ramona. We'll see if she enjoys it as much as having brothers! The movie will be filmed in Vancouver, Canada, which Selena describes as her second favorite place in the world. She spent three months there filming *Another Cinderella Story* and so knows it quite well.

Selena is definitely on her way to realizing her dreams to become a successful actress, and she has gone about it with real determination and drive. From the time she was six years old, watching her mother onstage and helping her with her lines, to her most recent successes she has always known what she wants to do and has gone after her heart's desire. She has always had the support of her family, not only to help her get to auditions and to move with her to Los Angeles, but more importantly they have always made it clear that they will always be there for her. They have kept her grounded and have tried to keep her life as normal as possible. She told *Girls' Life*, "My mom is my best friend. She's always with me everywhere I go. Sometimes on set, I just need to see her face. I'm like, 'Mom, I need to see you.' I just have to have my mom." But Selena has also helped herself by being relaxed about her success, cherishing her accomplishments, and being grateful for the good luck that has come her way.

Her life seems very busy right now with all the television and movie work, not to mention the work on her forthcoming debut album. What is life like for Selena when she has a little time to herself?

 # Selena's Style & Beauty Tips

 Selena loves to be comfortable in her clothing, and is often seen in jeans. She glams them up for a big night out by wearing high heels and a fitted shirt.

 Her naturally curly, long dark hair is always gorgeous whether she wears it up in a simple bun or pulls it slick and straight. She and her hair always shine. She keeps Ted Gibson hairspray and a comb in her purse for touch-ups.

 She brings out the beauty in those big, brown eyes with some Maybelline mascara. For night time, she'll define her eyebrows more, and use darker eye colors.

 For lips she loves Carmex to keep chapped lips at bay and then uses Cover Girl's Wet Sticks for nice gloss and no thick layers.

 For daytime eyes she loves MAC's Naked Lunch—a pretty peachy color with a light shimmer.

 She enjoys the fragrance "Frilly Lilly," a light, fruity perfume with a classic edge.

She likes to hang out with her friends and listen to music or watch movies or go skateboarding. She loves to make treats and eat cookies, go shopping, or go to the beach. All the things that we all like to do. She is a very regular girl! One of her favorite ways to relax is to go surfing with her co-stars from *Wizards of Waverly Place*. In fact, it was Jake T. Austin who taught her —after he had done a surfing movie, *Johnny Kapahala, Back On Board*. She told PBSKids that "at first the ocean scared me a little bit, but we don't go too far out. Once you ride that first wave, there's something about it that keeps you riding more and more." And now she uses surfing as a way of leaving all the pressures of life behind, as stress relief. She recommends that everyone should find a sport or hobby to do just that. "Like with surfing, it's nice to go on a beach and just forget about stuff and get away. It's fun. And acting's kind of like a sport for me too, it's the same as something like football or basketball for other people. It's something you do

for fun and something you're serious about."
(PBSKids)

And of course she loves to hang out with her BFF, Demi. Demi told *Latina* magazine: "I'll meet other actors who are like, 'Let's go to a party.' But Selena and I would rather rent a horror movie and just eat pickles. That's our ideal sleepover." What's with the pickles? Apparently it's a Texas thing. In movie theaters there, people can buy pickles to snack on. It's something that both girls miss. At Selena's Sweet 16 birthday party (which had a Mad Hatter/Alice in Wonderland Theme) she even had a pickle bar!

Demi and Selena have been friends for almost ten years, and it doesn't seem that their new lives are going to change that any time soon. They like to talk to each other on the phone a lot, for two hours at a time, and when they are away from each other filming in distant locations it is really hard on them. What does Demi have to say about Selena? She told *People* magazine, "It's just crazy to realize that Selena and I have known each other almost our entire lives. I can totally go to her with any problem and she will not judge me, no matter what. I can trust her with anything, and she can trust me. We'll definitely take each others' secrets to the grave."

It is well-known that Selena was determined that her friend Demi would be noticed by Disney executives and told her about as many auditions as she could. But she went one step further. One day during a pause in the taping of *Wizards of Waverly Place* she called her friend up from the audience and brought her onto the stage. Once there, Demi made the most of her opportunity and sang Christina Aguilera's *Ain't No Other Man* with so much fire that all the Disney executives turned their heads. She had their attention all right! Soon after that Demi got another great breakthrough and was cast in *Camp Rock* along with the Jonas Brothers. Now that's a good friend! And Selena couldn't have been happier for Demi. Of course, she would get to meet the Jonas Brothers too.

Selena loves to hang out with her mom. Her mom is her number one role model because she has always been so supportive of her. She told PBSKids, "I always go to my mom for advice." At one point in her life, when Selena was beginning to deal with having fans and fan sites devoted to her, she became upset about all the rumors that would float around about her—often about her and her friendship with Demi. Her mother gave her excellent, down-to-earth advice and taught her daughter not to take everything personally. Now she doesn't, and she is able to view the things she reads about herself —and about other stars—a lot more objectively. As Selena is away from home a lot, she especially appreciates time with her mom and step-dad when she is back. They enjoy quiet time together, often just hanging out in sweat pants, eating junk food, and watching movies.

And what about boyfriends? Beautiful Selena has been linked with several crush-worthy guys including Cody Linley, Taylor Lautner, and

Nick Jonas, but she always likes to keep that side of her life quite private, saying that they are just friends. She has always had guy friends ever since she was little, partly because she was a tomboy and also because she finds guys more down-to-earth, less "omigod" dramatic. One of her best friends is a boy that she grew up with in Texas, Randy Hill, who owns a skate shop.

Check it out!

Her perfect guy "wears Converse, is totally laid-back, and doesn't worry about being cool."

Who are the actors that inspire Selena, other than Barney the purple dinosaur of course? She has always loved Judy Garland in *The Wizard of Oz*, especially singing "Somewhere over the Rainbow."

It was the first song that Selena ever learned to sing. But her role model as an actress is Rachel McAdams. As she told PBSKids, "I fell in love with her in the movie *Mean Girls*. I love how she spreads herself out. She reinvents herself each time, and that's what I respect and love about her the most." Selena has often said that Shia Leboeuf is her celebrity crush and that she would love him to come onto the *Wizards of Waverly Place* as a guest star, but it's not clear if it's his acting that inspires her…. She is also a huge Johnny Depp fan and admires the broad range of his work and the chances he has taken as an actor. His talent for choosing great scripts is definitely inspiring.

Selena helps out!

Selena has made a reputation for herself because of her genuine kindness—to her family, her co-stars, and her friends. It is no surprise that her clean-cut, hard-working image has attracted several charity organizations. In the fall of 2008, she was named as a spokesperson for the children's charity UNICEF to take part in their Trick or Treat Campaign. Her role was to help kids understand the importance of Unicef's work in helping disadvantaged children around the globe. On accepting her leadership role, Selena said, "I want to help encourage other kids to make a difference in the world." She was chosen, according to Unicef's president Caryl Stern, because "young people can relate to Selena, and she is a great role model who we believe will greatly enhance the visibility of the program."

Selena does see herself as a role model and takes this part quite seriously. She told *Extra*, "[Being famous] is overwhelming and there's a lot to think about...to know there are hundreds of kids out there that look up to me. I know that's a big responsibility. I am also very confident to say that it is wonderful and I'll do my best that I can do to be the best role model I can be."

For much of the second half of 2008, Selena was connected with the organization UR Votes Count which gave teens a chance to make their voices heard through a nationwide campaign that went to 150 malls in 42 states and gave teens the opportunity to vote on key issues: such as education, the economy, the Iraq war, and the environment as well as to vote for the next US president. Selena's after-election comments can be found on the UR Votes Count Web site: "It's incredible so many teens came out to vote and learn more about the issues facing our nation today. I'm so proud to have been able to lend a hand in helping to educate my peers and usher in this next generation of voters."

Selena is also involved in getting teens to drive safely and has filmed a couple of safety commercials for State Farm Insurance. They air on the Disney Channel. Her advice in the commercial? "Being a safe driver means not taking any chances. Always wear your seat belt and pay attention to the speed limit. Don't text or talk on the phone while driving. Who doesn't love to text? But I can wait." This is obviously a subject close to her heart as even before she passed her driving test she stood in the rain at a DUI (Driving under the Influence) checkpoint in Los Angeles to watch local law enforcement take action against drivers who they thought were driving drunk. "I just want to get educated. Drunk driving is obviously a serious issue that we all need to be aware of."

Another project close to Selena's heart (and now close to mine) is her work with Island Dog and DoSomething.org (for whom she is an animal activist spokesperson). While she was filming *Princess Protection Program* in Puerto Rico, she became aware of a real problem with abandoned and homeless dogs on the Caribbean island, and, as she has always been a dog lover, she wanted to do something to help. She told *Latina* magazine, "We noticed all of these stray dogs and puppies. We ended up finding out that Puerto Rico has a 'dead dog beach.' It sounds worse than it is but people actually kill dogs for fun here."

Check it out!

Selena is a dog lover and has four dogs as pets, including Chip whom she adopted from an animal shelter.

Selena found out that there are over 200,000 dogs (and cats) roaming the streets and beaches of Puerto Rico suffering from illness, starvation, and abuse. When she was over in Puerto Rico again filming the *Wizards of Waverly Place* movie she was able to do something about the problem. She said in a blog entry, "This time around I'm teaming up with DoSomething.org and my mom, Brian (my stepdad), David (Henrie), Jake (Austin), David (DeLuise) are all going to help out today along with some of my crew from set! We are spending the day feeding puppies, washing them and hanging out with them. After we spend the day with them we are sending these dogs to different places in the U.S, the no-kill dog shelters so they can find a home." She also filmed a moving 'dog'-umentary on the beach to promote awareness of the problem. Next, she got in touch with her friends (members of band Forever the Sickest Kids, Taylor Swift, and Corbin Bleu) and teamed up with Charity Buzz. They donated items to an auction, the proceeds of which will benefit Island Dog, Inc. Selena is one busy, motivated person!

What's next?

And what about her future? She has said that she would like to continue to challenge herself in her acting and take on a wide range of roles. She would love to play a mean girl, "the bad person." She has even mentioned that she might like to act in a horror movie because she loves to watch them. Now that would be fun. I think we're going to be seeing her around for a long time. As you can see,

Selena Gomez has a great, down-to-earth personality, and Demi Lovato is lucky to have her as a BFF.

And by the way, if you know anything about who donated money to Selena's charity auction and won me a pair of Converse sneakers, I'd be very interested to have that scoop!

PART THREE
Games & Quizzes

So, you think you know Selena?

1. Which song do Selena and Demi sing along to when they do their famous secret handshake?
   a. *Barney* theme song
   b. "The Wheels on the Bus"
   c. "Gimme a Break" KitKat jingle
   d. Chili's baby back ribs jingle

2. What is the name of Selena's favorite sports team?
   a. Dallas Mavericks
   b. Texas Rangers
   c. Dallas Cowboys
   d. San Antonio Spurs

3. What is Selena's favorite fruit?
   a. Mango
   b. Orange
   c. Peach
   d. Apple

4. What is her favorite school subject?
   a. Math
   b. Science
   c. Music
   d. Drama

5. How tall is Selena?
   a. 5'5"
   b. 5'8"
   c. 5'2'
   d. 5'10"

6. What is Selena's Chinese astrological sign?
   a. Year of the Ox
   b. Year of the Tiger
   c. Year of the Snake
   d. Year of Monkey

7. What was the name of the middle school that Selena attended in Texas?
   a. Danny Jones MS
   b. Fulmore MS
   c. West Ridge MS
   d. Marshall MS

8. What does Selena's name mean?
   a. It means "loved one" in Spanish
   b. It means "moon" in Greek
   c. It means "flower" in Arabic
   d. It means "wisdom" in Latin

9. What does Selena like to do best in her spare time?
   a. Go to music concerts with her friends
   b. Work out at the gym
   c. Take cooking lessons
   d. Stay home and rent movies

10. Which are Selena's two favorite Paramore songs?

    a. "Fences" and "Born for This"

    b. "That's What You Get" and "Fences"

    c. "Misery Business" and "All We Know"

    d. "Born for This" and "Decoy"

11. What secret talent has Selena revealed?

    a. Being able to touch the tip of her nose with her tongue

    b. The ability to learn foreign languages quickly

    c. Spitting gum in the air and catching it in her mouth

    d. A near-photographic memory

12. What was one of the scariest things Selena says she has done?

    a. Learning to surf

    b. Eating quail eggs

    c. Sky diving

    d. Taking fencing lessons

13. One Halloween Selena was planning as dressing up as a celebrity (but didn't in the end). Who was it?
    a. Captain Jack Sparrow
    b. Taylor Swift
    c. Hannah Montana
    d. Hermione Granger

14. What unusual food does Selena like to eat every day?
    a. Salt
    b. Lemons
    c. Onions
    d. Cucumbers

15. How many *Harry Potter* books had Selena read before filming *Wizards of Waverly Place*?
    a. Seven
    b. Two
    c. None
    d. Three

16. If Selena could switch places with one person who would it be?
    a. Rachel Bilson
    b. Demi Lovato
    c. Sarah Michelle Gellar
    d. Her mom

17. What is Selena's favorite TV show?
    a. *One Tree Hill*
    b. *Wizards of Waverly Place*
    c. *90210*
    d. *Gossip Girl*

18. What is one of Selena's favorite movies?
    a. *Transformers*
    b. *Hannah Montana: The Movie*
    c. *Mean Girls*
    d. *Pirates of the Caribbean*

19. Who was Selena talking about when she said "I'll be nice to them if they'll be nice to me."
    a. Her co-stars on *Wizards of Waverly Place*
    b. The Jonas Brothers
    c. Disney executives
    d. The paparazzi

20. If Selena were president which issue would she educate kids about more?
    a. The economy
    b. Global warming
    c. Education
    d. Healthcare

Best Friends Quiz

Selena and Demi are true BFFs. How does your friendship with your BFF rate? Take the quiz below and see.

1. You're having a bad day and can't face going out to the movies as planned with your BFF.
    a. Does your BFF not seem to mind and agrees to go the next night?
    b. Does she get mad at you and tell you she's going to go with somebody else if you don't go?
    c. Does she show up at your house with your all-time fave DVD and a tub of your fave ice cream?

2. When it's your birthday party does your BFF...
    a. Spend the evening hanging out with your little cousins?
    b. Insist on following you around, sitting next to you, and hogging you the whole evening?
    c. Have an awesome time with all your guests, then help you blow out the candles on your cake?

3. You're excited about going bowling tomorrow with some friends, including your crush, but when you look in the mirror you see a huge pimple sprouting on your forehead. When you get dramatic and beg for your BFF's advice, does she...

a. Say, "What pimple?" and change the subject?

b. Agree with you that it is hideous, suggest you stay home tomorrow, and offer to entertain your crush for you?

c. Call her Grandma in Peru to ask for her special recipe for vanishing cream, then dash into the kitchen to whip up the remedy?

4. You get the worst grade you've ever had at school, and you're scared you'll be grounded for a year. Does your BFF...

a. Say, "What's the big deal, it's only science?"

b. Suggest you ask your crush for extra tutoring and then reveal he's been helping her all year?

c. Offer to come over and be around while you break the news to the 'rents because they won't yell while she's there?

5. You stumble in the lunchroom and drop your tray of food all over the feet of your crush. You stutter in embarrassment while your BFF...

   a. Walks away to get some fries thinking this is a good time for you and your crush to be alone.

   b. Runs off in hysterics, shrieking that you got food all over her too.

   c. Laughs it off and helps you clean up.

6. Your BFF tries out for the school play, *Guys and Dolls*, and wins a part in the chorus line. When you congratulate her does she...

   a. Say thanks, and talk about how cool the other people are in the production and how busy she'll be with rehearsals?

   b. Storm away from you because she wanted the lead role, not a mini-part as a dancer?

   c. Hug you and tell you she's so excited for you to see her in the production?

7. You almost blow up the science lab doing a chemistry experiment and manage to singe your eyebrows half off. Does your BFF...

   a. Say they look much better now—they were always too bushy before?

   b. Say you've ruined her life by being such a klutz, and she'll only be your friend again when your eyebrows have grown back?

   c. Make you laugh and see the funny side of the situation—and lend you her special eyebrow pencil?

8. When your crush comes over to your group of friends and says, "Hi," and all you can do is stare and make a strange, gargling noise at the back of your throat, does your BFF...

   a. Try to make things better by shouting, "Way to go, Toad Throat?"

   b. Ask your crush for his cell phone number. For you, of course?

   c. Come to your rescue, offer you a cough drop, and say, "I'll be so glad when your laryngitis is gone?"

9. You tell your BFF something personal. The next day, you hear another friend talking about it. You feel hurt and confused. When you talk to your BFF about the way you feel, does she...

   a. Say, "You never said it was secret, so what's the big deal?"

   b. Fly off the handle and get mad because you've accused her of spreading gossip and doubting her friendship?

   c. Admit that what she did was wrong and apologize, and promise never to do it again?

10. It's your birthday, and your BFF is throwing a surprise party for you. Does she...

    a. Invite everyone and their grandmother, except those two "it" girls who seem to have their eye on her crush?

    b. Make a guest list of just your coolest friends and have them invite their cool friends, especially if they're cute guys?

    c. Invite everyone you like, even the nerdy guy in math class and your weird friends from the skate park?

11. You've decided to take trapeze lessons and you want your BFF to take them too. Does she...

    a. Say there's no way she's going to do that and then invite you to do jazz dance with her instead?

    b. Ask whether it's a good idea for you to be seen in public wearing leggings?

    c. Admit she's afraid of heights but she'll come along with you to watch the first lesson?

12. It turns out that you and your BFF both have a crush on the new guy in school. Does she...

    a. See which one of you he likes best and take it from there?

    b. Turn nasty and fight over him, and find ways to put you down in front of him?

    c. Laugh about it and say it makes sense that you both like the same things?

13. You're chosen as a "buddy" for a new girl in school. Your 'rents invite her over for dinner, and she gives you a friendship bracelet. You wear it so as not to hurt her feelings. The next day does your BFF...

   a. Stare at the bracelet but not mention it, then sit with other friends at lunch?

   b. Behave badly towards the new girl and start mean rumors about her?

   c. Ask about the bracelet, then chat with the new girl at lunch?

14. You're at the mall shopping with your BFF. You try on a new outfit and aren't sure if it's right for you so ask her opinion. Does she...

   a. Say, "Thank goodness you've finally found something, and can we go and eat now?"

   b. Totally put you down and tell you that you look terrible in it, then sneak back at the end of the day to buy it for herself?

   c. Tell you that she doesn't think the outfit is right for you, but then searches high and low to find you something else that is just perfect?

Selena Character Quiz

With Selena's awesome acting skills, she can play a variety of characters. See which Selena character you would be!

1. How do you act around boys?
   a. Very confident
   b. A little insecure
   c. You feel like you could get any boy to like you
   d. Depends on the day

2. What clothing style do you prefer?
   a. Trendy but casual
   b. Artsy and creative
   c. You enjoy dressing up
   d. A bit of a tomboy

3. You would describe yourself as:

   a. Mischievous; you like to rebel

   b. Helpful; you are down to earth

   c. Self confident; sometimes, your confidence may come off as being arrogant

   d. Opinionated; you're not afraid to stand up for yourself

4. What is your relationship like with your best friend?

   a. She is often tries to keep you out of trouble

   b. She always encourages you to step outside your comfort zone

   c. You are very independent and don't really have a best friend

   d. She is the complete opposite of you

5. How is your family life?
   a. You and your siblings have a strong bond and a playful relationship
   b. Your siblings treat you poorly and constantly pick on you
   c. You are an only child
   d. You have strict parents

6. When it comes to your hometown…
   a. You grew up in a big city
   b. You grew up in the suburbs
   c. You moved around a lot
   d. You are from a very small town

7. Which activity would you enjoy most?
   a. Shopping
   b. Dancing
   c. Singing
   d. Working

8. When it comes to advice…
   a. Your friends always come to you
   b. You always go to your friends
   c. You may think you know everything, but no one else does
   d. You and your friends exchange advice evenly

9. Your best friend is…
   a. Smart and sort of dorky
   b. Ambitious and artsy
   c. You are your own best friend
   d. A bit of a princess sometimes

10. What kind of smart are you:
    a. Street smart
    b. Art smart
    c. Manipulative smart
    d. Book smart

Harlee Harte

 # Which is the Perfect Pooch for You?

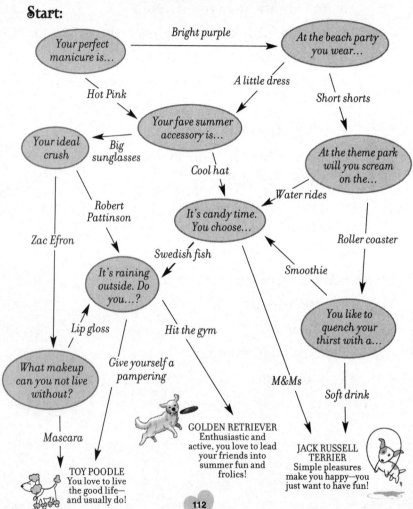

Start:

Your perfect manicure is…

— Bright purple → At the beach party you wear…

— Hot Pink → Your fave summer accessory is…

At the beach party you wear…
— A little dress → Your fave summer accessory is…
— Short shorts → At the theme park will you scream on the…

Your fave summer accessory is…
— Big sunglasses → Your ideal crush
— Cool hat → It's candy time. You choose…

Your ideal crush
— Zac Efron → What makeup can you not live without?
— Robert Pattinson → It's raining outside. Do you…?

At the theme park will you scream on the…
— Water rides → It's candy time. You choose…
— Roller coaster → You like to quench your thirst with a…

It's candy time. You choose…
— Swedish fish → It's raining outside. Do you…?
— M&Ms → JACK RUSSELL TERRIER

You like to quench your thirst with a…
— Smoothie → It's candy time. You choose…
— Soft drink → JACK RUSSELL TERRIER

It's raining outside. Do you…?
— Lip gloss → What makeup can you not live without?
— Hit the gym → GOLDEN RETRIEVER
— Give yourself a pampering → GOLDEN RETRIEVER

What makeup can you not live without?
— Mascara → TOY POODLE

GOLDEN RETRIEVER
Enthusiastic and active, you love to lead your friends into summer fun and frolics!

JACK RUSSELL TERRIER
Simple pleasures make you happy—you just want to have fun!

TOY POODLE
You love to live the good life—and usually do!

112

Help Selena and Demi get to the beach

All About Selena Gomez

See if you can find all 19 words hidden here. They might be written forwards, backwards, vertically, horizontally or diagonally. Good luck!

```
G O R S A N P U R J Q D O A P
S D T L U J O E M U G E G N D
W K E A B R V T I B H N M I Z
T X A D V O F N R X B I I T G
A E N T L O C I B O Y M S A K
T D X G E E L A N E H R C L J
L G O A A B R I N G F E H W B
B D Y N S N O S M I W T I M J
H R E G E L I A J E U E E P E
V R D Y J D Z B R G D D V I A
A Y Q D R A Z I W D C H O C N
F R I E N D L Y N E I B U K S
H T R A E O T N W O D N S L B
U N I C E F K F H P H C G E A
F D Q J U D X G J W N B A S Z
```

ALEX

BARNEY

DEMILOVATO

DETERMINED

DISNEY

DOGLOVER

DOWNTOEARTH

FRIENDLY

HORTON

JEANS

LATINA

MISCHIEVOUS

PICKLES

QUINCEANERA

SKATEBOARDING

SURFING

TEXAS

UNICEF

WIZARD

Selena's Scrambled Songs

Unscramble the tiles to reveal the titles of the songs and write the answers in the blank tiles. Remember each tile has three letters on it (a space counts as a letter).

1. Selena works her magic in this song…

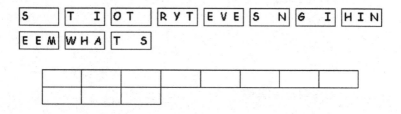

| S | T I | OT | RYT | EVE | S | NG | I | HIN |

| EEM | WHA | T S |

2. Selena sprinkles some fairy dust with this one…

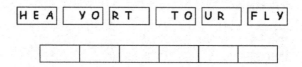

| HEA | YO | RT | TO | UR | FLY |

116

3. Selena wants to reach for the stars...

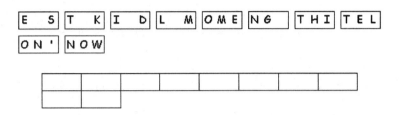

The next two song titles only have two letters (or letter and a space) on each tile.

4.   Selena is pretty mean here...

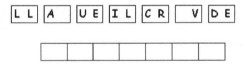

5. Selena is in love and wants the world to know...

All About Selena Gomez Solution

```
+ O + S A N + + R + Q D + A +
S + T L U + O E + U + E + N +
+ K E A + R V T I + + N M I +
T X A + V O F N R + + I I T +
+ E + T L O C I B O Y M S A +
+ + X G E E L A N E H R C L +
+ + O A A B R I N G + E H + +
+ D + N S O S M + + T I + J
+ + E + E + I A + E + E E P E
+ R + Y + D + + R + D D V I A
A + + D R A Z I W D + + O C N
F R I E N D L Y + + I + U K S
H T R A E O T N W O D N S L +
U N I C E F + + + + + + G E +
+ + + + + + + + + + + + S +
```

(Over,Down,Direction)

ALEX(5,1,SW)

BARNEY(9,5,SW)

DEMILOVATO(11,10,NW)

DETERMINED(12,10,N)

DISNEY(6,10,NE)

DOGLOVER(2,8,NE)

DOWNTOEARTH(11,13,W)

FRIENDLY(1,12,E)

HORTON(11,6,NW)

JEANS(15,8,S)

LATINA(14,6,N)

MISCHIEVOUS(13,3,S)

PICKLES(14,9,S)

QUINCEANERA(11,1,SW)

SKATEBOARDING(1,2,SE)

SURFING(4,1,SE)

TEXAS(1,4,SE)

UNICEF(1,14,E)

WIZARD(9,11,W)

Answers:

So, you think you know Selena?

Answers: 1. c, 2. d, 3. a, 4. b, 5. a, 6. d, 7. a, 8. b, 9. d, 10. a
11. c, 12. b, 13. c, 14. b, 15. c, 16. a, 17. d, 18. d, 19. d, 20. b.

Best Friends Quiz

Answers:

MOSTLY As

You need to think about what you want from a friendship and question whether your BFF is really a good friend to you. She doesn't always seem to be on your wavelength, or to have your best interests at heart. She's not outright mean to you, but with her clumsy handling of social situations and her back-handed compliments you have to watch out. She's a friend to you, but she doesn't have the commitment to be a true BFF.

MOSTLY Bs

You are in a friendship with a self-centered drama queen, which is not a good thing for you. This friendship is all about her: her whims, her needs. Sometimes she's jealous and clingy, and sometimes she'll stab you in the back then make you feel everything is all your fault. She may be fun to be with, the life of the party maybe, but she needs to learn a thing or two about friendship. You need her to give you space and trust otherwise you should walk away and find a real BFF.

MOSTLY Cs

You are very lucky. You have a loyal BFF who loves hanging out with you, even on your bad days, and will support you and laugh with you—just as you do for her. This is a balanced friendship filled with honesty and trust. You have a true friend who gets who you are, even in your worst moods, and best of all she will stand by you. Hold onto her!

Selena's Scrambled Songs

Answers: 1. Everything Is Not What It Seems, 2. Fly To Your Heart,
3. Tell Me Something I Don't Know, 4. Cruella de Vil, 5. Bang A Drum

Answers:

Selena Character Quiz

Answers:

MOSTLY As

You are Alex Russo from Wizards of Waverly Place. Alex is mischievous, spunky, and clever, always concocting different plans. Consequently, her best friend, Harper, is constantly trying to keep her out of trouble. Despite teasing her siblings, Alex is very close to her family. She loves shopping and dresses in a trendy style. A confident girl, she has no problem asking boys out. She grew up in a big city on the east coast and is street smart.

MOSTLY Bs

You are Mary Santiago from Another Cinderella Story. Mary is a down to earth girl who is always willing to help. Unfortunately, her step sisters tend to pick on her and make her life miserable. Luckily, she has an amazing best friend, Tami, who always guides her in a positive direction. Tami also encourages her to overcome her insecurities around boys. Mary is also very ambitious and strives to win a prestigious dancing scholarship.

MOSTLY Cs

You are Mikayla from Hannah Montana. Mikayla is a pop star and Hannah's biggest rival. She thinks highly of herself, which some people sometimes interpret as arrogance. She can also be two-faced and pretends to be friends with Hannah in public while being mean to her face. At the same time, Mikayla can be very open-hearted, and befriends Miley without realizing that Hannah is her alternate ego.

MOSTLY Ds

You are Carter Mason from the Princess Protection Program. Carter grew up in a small town. Her dad, a military man, is very strict. She dresses and acts like a tomboy, which is the complete opposite of her eventual best friend, Rosie, who acts like a princess. That's because she is one! Even though the two girls are different, they complement each other well.

Giving Back and Feeling Good

Just like Harlee and the gang, many stars help give back to the community through their involvement with charities. Check out some of the charities young celebrities help:

Selena Gomez contributed to UNICEF, a charity that helps less fortunate children around the world. She also auctioned herself off for Rosie O'Donnell's charity, which "supports the intellectual, social, and cultural development of disadvantaged children throughout the United States."

Taylor Swift has been involved in over a dozen charities! She really enjoys donating. Donations included her prom dress to donatemydress.org, $10,000 to the St. Jude Children's Research Hospital, $100,000 to Red Cross, the truck her record company gave her for her birthday, and part of the proceeds from her merchandise sales.

The Jonas Brothers are so committed to helping out that they even started their own charity. They donate 10% of their earnings ($1.2 million and counting!) to the Change for Children Foundation. The money then goes to other charities, including the American Diabetes Foundation, the St. Jude Children's Research Hospital, and Summer Stars: Camp for Performing Arts.

Taylor Lautner designed a one-of-a-kind, signed, messenger bag that was auctioned off to support the charities Books for Kids and The Children's Place.

Robert Pattinson auctioned off a couple of kisses to support the group amfAR's Cinema Against AIDS. When the bidding finished, two people had agreed to pay $20,000 each for the chance to kiss the *Twilight* hottie!

There are many ways you can help those in need, just like your fave teen celebrities. Here are a few ideas to get you started in your community:

Animal shelters: Many animals sadly don't have homes. You can volunteer at animal shelters and help improve their quality of life.

State parks: State parks need help staying beautiful. Volunteer to help out with a wide range of things, from trail maintenance to educational programs.

Food banks: Food banks collect food and give it to people who cannot afford to purchase it. Help serve poor people in your community, especially around the holidays.

Homeless shelters: Like food banks, homeless shelters need help serving people with meals and other services.

Habitat for Humanity: This program helps build houses for people in need. Habitat for Humanity even schedules trips to other countries during school breaks, so you and your friends can make a difference while traveling somewhere new.

Libraries: Libraries need volunteers to help with a variety of tasks, including shelving books, reading to kids, and running special programs.

Senior Citizen Centers: Senior citizens would love the friendship of a younger person. The centers also often run community activities.

Environmental organizations: There are many groups that help out the environment. Participate in activities such as cleaning up beaches or leading recycling drives.

Sports programs: A variety of sports programs are run by volunteers. From basketball to cheerleading, the help of teen coaches is often needed.

Red Cross: This organization offers help to people who have encountered emergencies. Donate blood, rebuild houses, or participate in a number of other activities with the Red Cross.

Check out the Internet for more information on the suggestions above.

Harlee Harte is a fictitious junior at Hollywoodland High School. She is the celebrity columnist for her school's student newspaper, where she writes the column "HarteBeat."